CW00853020

Santa Baby, Maybe

A Sophie Mays Novel

SANTA BABY, MAYBE

Text and Illustration Copyright © **2016 by Sophie Mays**

ISBN-13: 978-1541062290
ISBN-10: 1541062299

Publisher
Love Light Faith, LLC
400 NW 7th Avenue, Suite 825
Fort Lauderdale, FL 33302

This book is dedicated to all the people whose lives were touched by the Gatlinburg and Pigeon Forge wildfires.
This book was written just prior to the occurrence and is set in a fictional Tennessee town which overlooks the beautiful Great Smoky Mountains.
Our hearts and prayers go out to those whose lives were affected.

TABLE OF CONTENTS

Santa Baby, Maybe

A Christmas Story of Serendipity &
Silver Linings

Chapter 1.

Laid off. Those two words seemed to bounce back and forth, back and forth inside Colin's head. By themselves, each word was perfectly innocent, innocuous. But together, they became something devouring and lethal. They'd been eating at him all day, ever since he'd left his ex-boss's office four hours ago.

Welding school wasn't exactly cheap. He'd made an investment in his own future, and the bottom had fallen out of it. Laid off. What kind of company starts laying people off in November? A week before Thanksgiving? A month before Christmas?

Colin was sitting alone in the Starbucks near his former workplace. He didn't trust himself to get something stiffer to drink, not when his mood was dark as the cloudy autumn sky outside. An icy rain was lashing at the big windows and Colin sat staring out of them, thinking in circles and not getting nowhere.

What was he going to do now? The thought of burdening his family at this time of year by telling his father or his sister that he'd been let go was almost too much for even his caramel latte to smooth over. He took another sip, just in case, and turned the part of the cup with his name scribbled across it until it was hidden in his hand. If he could avoid being seen drinking sweet frou-frou drinks, it would help his mood. Everybody expected a guy in jeans and work boots to be drinking straight black coffee.

Of course, he might not be wearing work boots for long. Colin looked down at them sadly. With Christmas on the way, there was one market that was booming: retail. A shiver dropped down his spine. He hadn't worked retail in over fifteen years, since he was a kid in high school, but if a company as big as Hawthorne was letting go of welders, the market for his skill couldn't be good.

The wet afternoon outside looked especially bleak when he thought of that. How long had it been since he hunted for a job? Six years? Seven? He'd been on with Hawthorne since he started welding. Colin took another sip. He'd have to inquire at Frank & Sons, the only other big factory in the area. The sad thing was, being laid off when he was as skilled and well liked as he was, wasn't promising for a long and prosperous career anywhere else. His boss had raked his hands over thinning hair, audibly racked with guilt over having to let Colin go. They'd let several people go this week, many of them senior welders with excellent reputations. As he was told today, Hawthorne had new investors who wanted more laborers for less money, and the quickest way to achieve that was by letting go of some of their higher paid employees. Colin rolled his warm cup between his palms. Who knew that working his way up the ladder, working as hard and faithfully as he had, would end with him up being replaced by two younger, less experienced, and apparently way less expensive workers. At the moment it boggled his mind.

A woman in a J. Crew skirt suit opened the door, letting a blast of icy air in. Colin's chair was near the door and he got a face-full of November wind, thick with the smell of rain and cold. He waited for it to close, but she was struggling with her umbrella, which had gotten caught in the corner of the doorway. Other cozy occupants of the coffee shop were turning to look at her now as the seconds ticked and the chill began whipping through the room.

Colin set down his coffee and crossed the room to help her. "Here, ma'am," he held the door wide so her umbrella could detach. She got it free and smiled gratefully at him.

"Thank you," she said breathlessly. Her light-brown hair was smoothed into a perfect twist at the back of her head, but strands had blown free in the struggle with the umbrella. Her beige and red plaid scarf was askew, hanging not quite right around her slender neck.

"It's the worst thing about autumn, I swear. Umbrellas."

It was his turn to say something, but Colin just stood there, silent as a post, struggling to think of something charming to say to the gorgeous woman in front of him. He was definitely not use to face to face with someone as beautiful and refined looking on a daily basis.

"No problem," he answered finally. He waved awkwardly and retreated back to his seat by the door.

If his awkwardness bothered her, she didn't show it. Pulling off her scarf and leather gloves, he watched her walk up to the counter to order.

Colin sighed. As if he didn't feel useless enough.

His only comfort was the severance pay. After five years, employees at Hawthorne were entitled to ninety days severance benefits, so he had a little time to get a plan together. Of course, if he'd taken the supervisor promotion they'd offered back in May, he'd have six months' severance…

Colin had to clear that thought. He still had options and some time to act before things got dodgy. His Range Rover was paid off, at least. Thank goodness for small blessings. Three months' pay, and he was sure to find something between now and then. It was Friday. He'd take a day or two off to mope, and then he'd bounce back on Monday and be back to work before he knew it.

Better still, he'd already purchased Christmas presents for his family, so really his situation wasn't dire. Colin was that rare breed that stated he would buy Christmas gifts throughout the year for people, and then actually did it. He'd had gifts for his father, sister, brother-in-law, and his sister's two kids bought, wrapped, and stashed in the closet since September. The hardest part of gifting for Colin was having to wait until December 25th to give them.

The beautiful lady with the umbrella was

collecting her coffee now and heading back out the door. She gave Colin a friendly little smile on her way out, opened her umbrella without trouble, and walked off into the parking lot. Colin sighed and tried to focus on work.

He could still hardly believe it. Who hands out lay-offs the month before Christmas?! He took in a deep breath and tried to think. In some backwards way, maybe this was a blessing. It certainly didn't feel that way, but it had been proven more than once that sometimes there was a greater plan at work. He batted back and forth as to whether he should apply to Frank & Sons first thing Monday. His eyes rose to the wet parking lot. He stared out the hazy window not really looking at anything, but thinking again of the pretty brunette. Maybe he would take a little time before jumping right back into welding. He hadn't taken a day off in who knows how long. He had a few friends around town who might have some leads on odd jobs. Brandon worked building luxury homes up in the hills. Jack worked for a repair company. Jack's wife, Sarah, was helping put up a new apartment complex across town. Surely somebody had extra work to be done. Someone in Evanswood, Tennessee, was hiring, and Colin figured he could track them down one way or the other. He took a sip of his latte.

But first, he was going to be properly angry for at least another day.

Chapter 2.

It had been a long, intense day even before her umbrella got stuck in the door at Starbucks. By the time Nora got home, she was ready to kick off her heels and never get out from under the fuzzy blanket on her couch ever again. She hung up her umbrella, took off her scarf, coat and gloves, and walked past her neat kitchen into the living area. With a flip of a switch, the lights fluttered on.

She loved the condo that she owned, a

luxury unit settled on the banks of the Little River. Smoky Mountain National Park reared up in the dark distance outside her windows, with the twinkling lights of Evanswood shining below. In the low-hanging rain clouds and relentless downpour, even the mountains' shapes were gone in a wash of murky black. When the sun came up tomorrow, the brilliant fall colors would radiate brightly against the dawn sky. The view was one of Nora's favorite things about her condo.

She'd never even managed to finish her coffee, and now she poured the remainder of the pure black liquid down the sink before tossing the cup in the recycling bin and heading to her bedroom in search of pajamas. Her black business heels were left in the bottom of her closet with the good intention of putting them back on her shoe rack later, and her dry-clean-only suit went back on the hanger. She had a few things to be taken to the cleaners. It would probably have to be this weekend, unfortunately.

With a sigh, Nora realized that she'd left her briefcase in her car. If she'd realized earlier, Nora might have gone out to get it, but by now she was standing around her bedroom in her bra and panties. That ship had sailed she resigned. She didn't have any urgent cases pending, and if her firm really needed something, they could call her cell phone. The briefcase could wait out in the car until tomorrow.

Nora rifled through her purse to make sure that she'd at least brought her phone in. She had; there it was, sitting between her wallet and her chapstick. Definitely no need to go out into the cold again just to go retrieve the briefcase that she wasn't planning on using tonight. She dropped her purse on the bed and opened her dresser drawer to find a pair of pajamas.

With a tiny meow, a bundle of black fur squeezed out from under the bed.

"Oh, hello, Arty!" Nora scooped the cat up and into her arms. Artemis had only lived with her for two weeks, but he was already making himself at home in her quiet condo. It had only taken six months of living here alone before Nora had caved in and took a little visit to the local Humane Society. It turns out, November is a big month for black cats. The lady at the shelter admitted that their policy forbade adopting out black cats during October, just in case. Nora laughed, but also slightly shuddered at the implications.

Artemis was instructed to sit on the bed while Nora pulled on a set of warm flannel pajamas. She'd picked the red ones with leaping reindeer—Christmas was over a month away, but the cold fall weather put her in the holiday mood. The black cat followed her out into the living room where she pulled up the very fuzzy blanket she'd been dreaming of since the rain had started this afternoon.

A replay of the incident with the Starbucks door and the good-looking stranger unrolled in her mind, and Nora smiled. Well, rain was good for some things, at least.

It had been a long week. Nora worked with personal rights and domestic lawsuit cases, and it seemed like she was always exhausted by the time Friday rolled around. At this very moment, she needed badly to relax and forget her work week for a little while. She rubbed at the headache starting to throb at her temples. As her fingers kneaded into her hair it dawned on her that she'd forgotten to take it down. Artemis was disturbed by the movement, but Nora climbed off the couch and went into the bathroom to take the bobby pins out of her light brown bun. The release of tension brought a happy sigh to her lips.

"What should we watch, Artemis?" she

asked as she walked back into the den, hair falling around her shoulders. The little black tomcat had claimed a corner of the fuzzy blanket for himself and folded all his legs under his body. His yellow eyes were already closed. He ignored her, so Nora picked the remote up off the shelf without his input. "I think you're right. I've been in the mood to watch *Love, Actually*, too."

Chapter 3.

Colin was helping set the Thanksgiving table at his sister's house, setting out dishes and carefully stepping over children and dogs. Carol had a son and daughter who were so similar in age, appearance, and temperament that it was hard to tell them apart when they were wrestling around the house. To anyone not knowing better the assumption would be that they were twins. Colin told the rowdy duo for the hundredth time not to trip him.

They responded in unison, each clinging to one of his legs and laughing madly.

"Hey! Your mom isn't going to like it when I throw you both out in the rain with the dogs!" Colin told them. With exaggerated effort, he walked around the table, setting out plates and silverware, dragging the kids along and driving the two of them wild.

"Colin! Stop getting them worked up!"

"Yeah, Colin," Andrew agreed, chuckling. It had taken a couple years, but Colin liked Carol's husband Andrew now. Andrew reached down and pulled one of the giggling children off Colin—it turned out to be the boy, five years old and with his mother and sister's bright red hair. "Ben! Come on, now. Uncle Colin's trying to help, unlike you and your sister."

Once it was one-to-one, Colin had the upper hand and managed to pry his niece Jenny away. Benny and Jenny. Colin couldn't believe his sister hadn't noticed that the short forms of Benjamin and Jennifer rhymed.

"Any luck with the job hunt?" Andrew asked, as Ben wriggled away and six-year-old Jenny raced after him.

Colin shook his head. "Not yet. I thought I might find something through a buddy of mine, but at the moment nothing's really out there. Construction usually slows down in the winter, but this year something is definitely up. I'm down to looking at seasonal work."

"Did you try Frank's yet?"

Colin winced. Of course Andrew would say that first. Truthfully, Colin hadn't applied at Frank & Sons just yet. If nothing else came up he'd go to them, but Colin was going to exhaust his other options first. He ran a hand through his thick hair, and twisted his mouth in a frown.

"I haven't heard about any openings from them," Colin replied. It wasn't a lie. "But I'll probably be giving them a call in the next couple weeks."

"I still can't believe it," Carol muttered, carrying dishes in from the kitchen. They were covered with tin foil, but Colin smelled sweet potatoes and gravy. "After you've worked at Hawthornes for what, seven years? Happy Thanksgiving, here's a severance package. Nice."

It was exactly how Colin felt, but Carol always had a way of being angrier at other people's problems for them. He followed her into the kitchen to help carry out dishes. "Here, let me help with that. Where's Dad?"

"He's with Abby," Carol sighed, brushing hair off her forehead with the back of her wrist. "You should probably tell him dinner's about ready."

"Hey," Colin elbowed her. Carol looked up at him with her mouth pressed into a line. Colin made the same face back at her, and she laughed reluctantly. "I'll be fine. There's something in this town for me. I'm set for a couple months, either way."

She elbowed him back and nodded. "Yeah, I know. At least you don't have kids or anything."

Colin looked around at the chaos of Carol's household, the children rolling around on the floor, the dogs yipping and wagging their tails and knocking things off the coffee table. Colin chuckled.

"Yeah, at least."

Their father was cloistered upstairs in the nursery with Carol and Andrew's last and youngest child. Baby Abigail was not really a baby anymore, she was turning two in January. She and her grandfather were putting together building blocks on the carpeted floor, enjoying the relative quiet in the safe zone where the other children and dogs couldn't climb over the stair guards.

George looked up and grinned when he saw his grown son in the doorway. "Is it that time already?"

Colin nodded, and George stood with Abby following suit. She toddled to the gated doorway then tuned to her grandfather and sweetly demanded, "Up!" He lifted her into his arms, and followed Colin back downstairs. George MacCullough had black hair once. It seemed like a long time ago to Colin. Back before Colin and Carol had grown up, and before their mom had passed away. Now, George's hair was gray, but he looked young again as he dodged around the shrieking children toward the table. He settled Abby in her high chair and pulled out a chair of his own.

Ever since Evelyn MacCullough had succumbed to congestive heart failure two years ago, the family always had holidays at Carol's house. CHF had an even more lethal ring to it than being laid off, but sitting here with his dad and his sister and the additions that had been tacked on over the years Colin had to concede that things weren't so bad. For the first time since leaving his former boss' office Colin felt calm.

George led them in a prayer over the meal. Benny and Jenny managed to sit still for the whole two minutes, and then the symphony of clanging plates and moving dishes began. Carol made one heck of a feast, and it took up nearly every inch of tabletop. She sat now with Abby's highchair between herself and her husband, coaxing mashed potatoes and cranberry sauce into the toddler's mouth with mixed success. The dogs got more of her food than Abby did.

After his first bite, Colin's phone started to ring. He yanked it out of his pocket and silenced it quickly. Whoever was calling, he wasn't interested right that minute.

As he made his way home that evening, he remembered the mid-dinner call and pulled out his phone.

"Hello?"

"Hi, I got a call from this number," Colin explained. It was pouring down sleet now. It was stupid to be on the phone, but no one else was out driving on Thanksgiving thankfully.

"Hey! Colin! It's me Jim."

"Jim? Why didn't your number come up on my phone?"

"Ah, well, I had to get a new one." Now that Colin had a name, he could recognize the voice. It had been a couple years since Jim quit working for Hawthorne. "The wife finally split. I had to change the phone plan."

After the candlelit contentment of his family on Thanksgiving, Colin tried to sound properly sorry. "That's too bad, Jim. Sorry to hear it."

"It's fine, it's fine. But I heard from Brandon that you had an eye out for work. You available in a couple hours?"

"What?" Colin eased to a stop at a red light; there was no one else at the intersection. "What do you have me doing in a couple hours?"

"I've been picking up a lot of odd jobs lately, and I'm working at the mall tonight putting up Christmas decorations. You know, the trees out in the parking lot, and the Santa meeting set-up thing. We need an extra guy, do you want to help out?"

"Um, yeah," Colin couldn't really say no. "Is this... you know... legitimate? Are we getting paid in cash, or what?"

"Paid in cash," Jim agreed. His tone sounded accompanied by a shrug.

The light was stuck on red. Colin inched

forward a little, trying to trip the sensor. "I guess. Can you send me a text with the place and time?"

"Yeah! Sure thing! I'll see you in a couple hours! Hey do you have any tools you can bring?"

Colin started to creep through the intersection. How long did he have to wait if the light was stuck? There was a legal time limit, but he couldn't remember. Five minutes?

"Yeah, what should I bring?"

"Just bring the whole toolbox. You never know what we might need."

His whole toolbox? Colin frowned. That was several hundred dollars' worth of equipment, just in his main box. Did Jim think he was going to bring all his good tools to a job with a bunch of guys getting paid in cash?

"I'll bring some—whoa!"

He hit the brakes as a car came cruising through the intersection. To be fair, they had the green, and they'd had to brake and veer to avoid getting scraped along Colin's grill. The little sedan laid on the horn and zoomed off.

That had been too close. Carol would strangle him if she ever found out, worrier that she was. "Hey, Jim, I've got to go, I'm driving. Send me that info." Finally, the light turned green on his side. Colin eased into motion, checking both ways twice after the close call. "I'll see you in a couple hours."

"You'll bring your tools?"

"Yeah, I'll bring some. Bye."

Chapter 4.

"Sorry I'm late," Nora called through the entryway of her parents' traditional two-story house. "It's raining like mad out there. And I almost hit some crazy person creeping through that stop light that never changes over on Maple Street."

"He would have been sorry," Nora's younger sister Becka replied smugly. Becka was just visible in a sweater and apron through the doorway, standing at her station behind the kitchen island. She was slicing up the turkey and stacking the steaming, juicy layers on one of the nice platters. Nora caught a nose full of the smell and felt her stomach growl. "Bad luck to get in a car accident with a lawyer," Becka continued.

"I don't even do motor vehicle collisions," Nora scoffed as she got her shoes off. She hung up her coat as her grandmother met her in the hall. "Hi, Grandma! How was your flight? Not too terrible?"

"Never too terrible to come visit for the holidays," Grandma Mullen answered. She enclosed Nora in a hug, even though, heels or no heels, Nora was easily a half a foot taller. "Besides. The cocktails are cheaper if you're flying on a holiday."

She laughed at the look on Nora's face and they followed the narrow hallway into the den. There, still in her apron, Nora's mother, Viv, sat sourly, watching the Turkey Bowl with her husband.

"Can you believe your sister has kicked me out of the kitchen?" Viv said at once, in obvious disapproval.

"Well, good," Nora replied. "Dad needs someone to watch the Turkey Bowl with since Mikey took that transfer to California."

Her father laughed and her mother pursed her lips, and Nora leaned over and gave each of them a hug and kiss on the cheek.

"Speaking of that, I cannot believe they wouldn't let your brother off for Thanksgiving," Viv huffed. "What kind of company does that?"

"Nora! Help me set the table!" Becka called from the kitchen, attempting to save her sister from their mother's impending rant.

"Nora just got here," Viv insisted.

"I'll help. It's no problem." Nora was already headed into the kitchen, where plates of food were stacked. "Where's Margaret? Off for Thanksgiving?"

"Yeah, she needed a couple days off." Becka had been loading squash, green-bean casserole, turkey, and boiled pearl onions onto plates and into bowls, but she didn't quite have the polish of someone who usually cooked for others. "Margaret offered to help out the first half of the day, since Grandma came this morning and all, but she should have the weekend off with her kids." Becka scraped the last of the carrots into a glass serving bowl before looking up accusingly at her sister. "Hey, I thought I told you to bring a boyfriend."

"I don't see you filling an extra seat at the table," Nora poked back. She had a dish in each hand, carrying them out to the big dining room table in the next room.

"I thought you were thinking of bringing that guy from your firm?" Becka ignored her comment, not letting the subject drop.

Becka sure had a good memory, Nora marveled, although she wasn't too pleased to admit it. She couldn't have mentioned that guy more than once or twice.

"Married."

"That sucks," Becka muttered. Five years younger than Nora, she still lived with their parents while she went to pharmacy school. Not that she was about to say it out loud, but Nora was secretly glad that Becka hadn't brought anyone. She knew that part of it was the threat of being upstaged by her little sister yet again. Becka was already notoriously better at finding men than her overworked older sister. Worse still, every time Becka came home with a new boyfriend, it triggered their mother to start making less than subtle comments about grandkids while looking longingly at Nora.

"Yeah. Though, I did have a handsome stranger save me from the doorway at

Starbucks last week," Nora chuckled. "Think I should have brought him?"

"Maybe. Was he cute?"

"He was...manly" Nora walked back into the kitchen, thinking. "Definitely didn't look like any of the lawyers I'm usually around. He had this dirty blond hair, and he was just... striking. You know?"

"No, I don't know."

"Like, his nose had probably been broken at some point and his jaw was really square. His features were almost rugged. Like a sexy lumberjack or something."

Becka squinted at her sister's awkward description.

"Like you know how Daniel Craig really doesn't have a classically handsome face, but it still works?"

Becka looked scandalized; she was digging stuffing out of the turkey, now, and stopped to put her hands on her hips, the large scooping spoon pointing accusingly in Nora's direction. "Daniel Craig *is* handsome, thank you very much." An exaggerated huff slipped out as she turned back to the stuffing.

"*Whatever,*" Nora mouthed.

By the time the family had gathered to say a prayer over their Thanksgiving meal, the smell of roast turkey, gravy, and the sharp tang of cranberry had everyone ready to eat. It was a fairly quiet dinner—after all, this was the first Thanksgiving without their animated brother here to dominate the conversation as he usually did.

Hours later, while she was dozing on the couch to the background noise of *A Christmas Story*, Nora tried to remember if there was anything that she really needed to wake up for tomorrow.

She groaned. She was going to be up early in the morning; her charity outreach to the children of the Evanswood Boys and Girls

Club had an event tomorrow. She had signed up to take the children out for some Christmas shopping. Nora had been looking forward to it all month, but now, falling asleep on her parents' couch, she wondered what on Earth she'd been thinking.

Chapter 5.

At one in the morning, Colin showed up in the
Northtown Mall parking lot to help put up
Christmas decorations. He'd packed his small
tool chest in the back of the Range Rover, but
he turned out to have worried for nothing. The
only guy who hadn't brought his own
equipment was Jim, who, of course, helped
himself to everything Colin had brought. Still,
Colin kept a sharp eye out. Jim was nice, in a
snake-oil salesman kind of way. Not the sort

of fellow that you depended on when it counted.

Not long after Colin arrived at the mall, the Black Friday shoppers starting to form their drowsy lines. Even the earliest stores weren't open for business until four a.m., but the diligent bargain hunters were camped out in increasing droves while Colin worked. By the time the crew finished up the next afternoon, Colin emerged from the mall to find the parking lot swamped with cars, and his Range Rover hidden in the sea of it. He began to wander up the isles in the vicinity of where he remembered parking.

The rising sound of children's voices sounded from the next aisle over. Colin stood tall to look over the row of SUVs in the way. A school bus with the words 'Evanswood Boys and Girls Club', had pulled into a block of open spaces near the back of the lot. A cadre of laughing grade-school kids hopped out, in matching shirts, herded by a pair of matching-shirted counselors and two—no, three—harried-looking volunteers.

The youngest volunteer caught his eye. Her light brown hair caught the gentle autumn sun and Colin recognized her instantly as the woman from Starbucks. She wasn't wearing a suit today, but her smoothly-styled hair was the same as it had been the day he first saw her. Today she was sporting dark, snug jeans and a soft-looking white cardigan. Even as she ran back and forth like a sheepdog trying to keep the excited children in line, her movements were graceful and precise.

Colin clicked his car key again, hoping he was close enough to hear the sound. Even if he still had a job, there was no way a woman like her would look twice at a welder. And an unemployed welder? With that, his chances were reduced to single digits.

The Rover honked from the next aisle over

and Colin headed toward the sound. Opening the back, he threw in his gear, closed it up and got in.

It was another beautiful November day. He'd been up all night, so Colin was only able to appreciate it in a hazy, sleep-deprived sort of way, but he took it in with appreciation. The Smoky Mountains were rising lazily over the edge of town. They burned with the vibrant orange-red of fall leaves, streaks of golden birches and red maples covering every inch. The sky above was the azure blue of pure lapis. It was the sort of day that felt wonderful and surreal, brimming with potential.

For Colin, however, the most he wanted out of the rest of the afternoon was to get home and collapse into bed. If his momentum held out, maybe he could manage a shower first, but that was about the extent of his ambition until he caught up on sleep.

Of course, when he parked in the drive that

cozied up against the side of his little house, Colin diligently unpacked his tools before the call of his sheets and warm quilt grew too great to ignore. He wanted to bring everything inside before he forgot. Colin balanced his tool chest on his thigh and unlocked the garage. The garage was the whole reason he'd bought this house. It was almost as big as the house itself, and he'd customized it into a workshop for his projects.

He dropped the box on the counter that ran along one entire wall of the workshop and turned to look at his most recent project in the light from the open door. He exhaled with shear exhaustion and set his hands on his hips. He scanned the workshop. Without work at Hawthorne, he'd had more time to tinker, and that wasn't the worst thing. His eyes landed on his current pre-occupation. A sculpture out of welded metal scraps, about waist height when it wasn't on a worktable. It had started out without purpose, but a mighty sturgeon with a hundred glimmering, mismatched scales had come to life, leaping out of metallic splashes of water.

Colin had no idea how he'd done it, but the one completed eye of the fish was intensely focused and seemed alive, no matter how you looked at it. The metal he'd fashioned it out of was a glimmering blue-silver, the color you imagined ice water must be, and shone with a stubborn brilliance, even though the rest of the sturgeon was made of metal that had been tarnished to varying degrees.

The impulse to cobble together scraps of metal had started years ago. At first he just wanted to practice his new craft. Then he found himself sitting down and creating things to wind down from a long week or to blow off steam. Colin had never been the artsy type, not in childhood, not in school. He couldn't remember ever creating a thing in any medium, not even scribbles in his notebooks as a kid. But the metal seemed pliant under his hands, willing to work with him to become something elegant, something remarkable even.

Colin sighed again, sleep tugging at his eyelids. Welding sculptures was well and good, but working on something to help pay his mortgage would have been preferable. He turned and headed out the workshop door, visions of his pillows taunting him all the way into the house.

Chapter 6.

As Black Friday wound to a close, Nora climbed into her car exhausted. She waved out the window to the children climbing on the playground equipment out in the yard at the Boys and Girls Club. She started up her engine and carefully reversed out of her parking spot. It was time for coffee and home, in that precise order.

It wasn't as if she had expected a field trip to the mall with two dozen grade school kids to be easy, but—having little experience with children, herself—Nora had underestimated the challenge of running twenty directions at once. The kids were supposed to be helping shop for the local church's toy drive; this was the first year the Boys and Girls Club had attempted this particular feat. Although the kids were surprisingly eager to think up ideas that other children might enjoy, their excitement over their mission made Nora's job feel like trying to control a herd of wayward goats.

The sun was getting low in the sky, but the sunrays were falling bright on the fiery mountains to the east. Autumn in Tennessee was long and gentle, but it was coming to an end in the next few weeks. The Smoky Mountains kept their intense colors for a good long run, but once December rolled in even the most stubborn trees had to let their leaves fall. The rainstorms of the last couple weeks had already begun stripping the colors from trees around town.

Nora decided to hit the drive-thru at Starbucks, and ordered her coffee black, as always. She tacked on decaf at the last minute, since she didn't want to be up the entire night, though she did need to read through some case files. There was an unholy line, but she sat patiently in her car. The muscles in her body slowly began to relax. It was nice to not be chasing children at the moment.

She glanced in the rear view mirror. Her briefcase was still sitting in the back. She'd left it in the car again last night in the rush to get from work to her parents' house. It was turning into a habit. For a second, Nora thought about bringing it up front and poking through a case file while she waited, but when she reached back the line moved and she dismissed the idea. There would be plenty enough time when she got home to review her deposition and the case details for when she met her client on Monday.

The cars inched forward again and Nora slowly idled forward with them. Her client on Monday afternoon was a custody battle of all things. She'd been involved with the case since last February, and she looked forward to the day it was filed away for good. It had begun with abuse allegations against the husband, which was something that no empathetic person ever looked forward to looking into. The wife had hired Nora to represent her, and had been so impressed with her work that when the divorce began, she asked Nora to represent her there, as well. The woman had been so admiring and grateful, Nora found it impossible to say no.

Nora pushed those thoughts aside. She'd been having a perfectly pleasant day until that popped into her head, and she was determined to go back to her happy place. At least until she got home and had to open the case file.

When she got to the window, Nora accepted her coffee, paid, and began her drive home. There were many advantages to being a lawyer, but there were plenty of times when a day full of herding rowdy children and helping the kids at the Boys and Girls Club's was much more appealing.

She volunteered at the club every week, reading to the kids, helping the staff, and just trying to give back in some way.

Of course, her out-of-office hours took an upshot at this time of year. There were work events and charity auctions, plus about a million other things that the Boys and Girls Club needed an extra hand with. In fact, next week she was helping with another field trip to the mall. The children were going to meet Santa.

Chapter 7.

Colin sat in his truck, the engine idling and smoke steaming up around the car. The temperature had taken a dip last night and today was a frigid one. The sun shone down on the frozen ground, kicking up the haze. In the distance was the main office of Frank & Sons. He saw a young man in Carhartts and a thick hoody pulled up over his head make his way from the front door out to an F150 parked in the lot.

The guy looked exactly how Colin imagined he looked not too many years back. Not quite ready to move, he continued his survey of the generic manila colored building. If he walked in that door, Colin was certain he would come out with a new job. He had a flawless reputation, gleaming references and a ton of experience. His fingers pinched his lips in thought.

As he stared, he saw his entire life lain out before him. Where he's been and where he would be heading, were exactly the same place. If he got the job, he'd have a good job with a steady paycheck. But as he'd just witnessed at Hawthorne, it was also naïve to think that he wasn't expendable. Any good person with the proper training could weld a pipe. When he had signed on a Hawthorne he had loved being part of a team, being loyal to a company; but when it came down to it, the loyalty in return was dictated by a lot more that mutual admiration. His supervisors loved him and in a perfect world would have never let him go; but they weren't the final word.

Another thought crossed Colin's mind as he watched the smoke puff out of the vents on the building. Was this all he was meant for? He wasn't providing for a family, he didn't need to clock in first thing in the morning and out in the evening day in and day out to please anyone. He had chosen this job, but he was a small part of a large machine, with no particular importance.

If he took a job at Frank & Sons, there was nothing to say that as soon as the economic tides turned again, he wouldn't find himself a little older, in another parking lot just like this one, having this same conversation.

Maybe it's worth gambling on himself. The words ran through his head. What did that mean exactly? He didn't really know, but the phrase repeated itself to him. He sat for several more minutes, looking at the building, looking at the grey-blue sky, and scanning the mountains off in the distance. For the first time in his life, the excitement of the unknown washed over him. He really didn't understand the words completely, but the idea of gambling on himself outweighed the lure of stability and a steady paycheck. Colin had always prided himself on being responsible and level-headed, but he couldn't help the feeling of adrenaline rushing thought him. He took a breath and tried to think as clearly as he could. He decided to give himself until the New Year to breath, pray, and just see if he still felt the same way on January 1st. It would be enough time to figure out if he was being crazy right now, and he knew perfectly well that he could get some sort of a job on January 2nd at Frank & Sons if he so desired.

Colin's breathing had picked up considerably

and it was all he could do to keep himself from tearing out of the parking lot in an epic cloud of dust. With the rest of the day free, he decided he would beeline to his favorite drive-through, get the froufiest frou-frou coffee he could and drive through the mountains, just enjoying the nature as God intended it.

Chapter 8.

Was that his alarm going off? Colin blinked awake, expecting to see sunlight seeping in around the curtains. But it was still dark outside, and it wasn't his alarm going off. It was his cell phone on the bedside table.

He flailed for the phone, knocking it onto the floor before he managed to follow the charging cable to its end. As quickly as he could, he hit 'answer'.

"Hey Colin!"

With a groan, Colin collapsed backward onto the bed. "Hi Jim."

"Hey—so I have another job you might want. Are you still looking?"

Where was Jim coming up with this work? Over the past week since the Black Friday job, he'd called twice, both with odds and ends of work that brought in a hundred or so bucks a turn. Colin had been eyeing Craigslist and the classifieds in the paper, and these odd jobs weren't listed in either place. Who did Jim know to get this insider info?

But so far, the police hadn't shown up to bust any illegal operations, so Colin kept taking the work Jim rustled up. His rounds of Evanswood associates hadn't yet turned up any other work for him.

"What's the job?" Colin managed to get the question out before a huge yawn cracked his jaw. He looked at the clock. It was four AM. Didn't Jim ever sleep?

"Well the Northtown Mall does that Santa thing for the kids, right?"

"Yeah… do they need something else put up for it?"

"Not exactly. I guess their guy that usually wears the suit on Tuesdays through Fridays backed out. You doing anything those days?"

Colin lay on his back, staring at the dark ceiling. At six-foot-something and two hundred pounds of muscle, Colin didn't exactly fit the Santa parameters. "Are you asking me if I want to be Santa?"

"Yeah."

Well, no beating around the bush there. Colin was about to ask where the heck he'd heard of this job, and why didn't he take it himself, but stopped. It was regular work, of a sort. At least through the month of December.

"Why not? When do they want me there?"

"Great! Just go to the mall office tomorrow by ten and tell them you're the guy Jim sent."

This sounded so sketchy. Colin sighed and agreed, and Jim hung up with a cheerful goodbye. When the phone was back on the bedside table, Colin turned over and tried to go back to sleep. The image of himself in a Santa outfit haunted him, however, and he tried to imagine what sort of looks he'd get from the mall staff tomorrow when he showed up for work. He was tall and muscular and relatively young, with hands like sandpaper. If they'd needed someone to dress up as a Viking or a lumberjack, he'd have been a better fit.

He couldn't have been asleep more than a half minute before the phone rang again. Colin scrambled for it blindly and picked up.

"Hello?"

"Hey, it's Andrew. Did I wake you?"

It was brighter in the room now. Colin looked at the clock. Six twenty-two. Six twenty-two, and his brother-in-law was calling to chat. "Yeah. What?"

"Sorry about the time. I'm headed to work, and I wanted to call you before I forgot again. I was talking to a friend last night about your sculptures and welding work."

"What about it?"

"My buddy's brother is getting married in January, and they're having some big engagement party in a couple weeks. He wanted to know if you could make something as an engagement present."

"In a couple weeks?"

"I know it's short notice. I told him so, but he wanted to talk to you. Is it okay if I give him your number?" To his credit, Andrew at least sounded sheepish, as if he was aware of how strange a time it was to be having this conversation.

Colin lay back again, thinking of the mass of metal pieces welded together in his workshop.

"Sure. Go ahead and tell him to call me."

Chapter 9.

The Northtown Mall was bursting with shoppers as Nora and Becka dodged from store to store. Nora always forgot to plan ahead, although every Christmas she swore to herself that she would buy gifts far ahead of time. It hadn't happened yet, and this year was no exception.

Nora was about to ask in desperation if their mother needed another candle for the bathroom, but Becka dragged her away from the Yankee Candle store before she could get it out.

"And how are you paying for gifts, anyway?" Nora asked suspiciously. She threw a pointed look at the new high-heeled boots Becka was wearing. They were cute, all right, but clearly fresh out of the box.

If Becka was even a little embarrassed, she didn't show it. "I've been saving up."

"Hmm." Nora tilted her head and raised an eyebrow, as if thinking. "Saving up what? Money you've begged off Dad? It seems a little backwards to be buying them gifts with their own money."

Becka pursed her lips in disapproval. "They don't mind and you know it."

They passed the Victoria's Secret. The Northtown Mall actually had two, and Nora had never been able to fully understand why. She had never even really looked, although Becka paused by the entrance. It wasn't as if she didn't have the money, but Nora didn't really see why she was suppose to have underwear that rivaled her clothes for attention. Maybe one day when she was married, but as it stood now, Artemis the cat wasn't really that picky about what she wore around the house.

"You could run up a two-thousand dollar shopping bill every month, and they'd tell you they didn't mind," Nora jokingly chided as they moved along. "Now that I've moved out and Mike moved to California, you know they'll do anything to keep you in the house as long as possible."

Becka didn't even bother trying to deny it. She nodded to the Santa meet-and-greet set up in the central atrium of the mall, a big winter cottage set-up with a fake gold and velvet chair set up and a big camera ready and aimed.

"I'm bringing the kids here tomorrow,"

Nora said, watching the next child in line approach the big Santa-suited man. The helper elves were hanging back, probably trying not to make the girl feel cornered. Nora couldn't imagine having a hundred strange children sitting on your lap all day—what a box of chocolates that must be. Not to mention the parents to go with. "I wonder how you keep your wits about you, doing that all day long," she wondered aloud.

"He's cute," Becka commented under her breath. Nora rolled her eyes.

"Into older men, now?"

"He can't be much older than you, really. He doesn't look old, under the beard. I wonder if he'd let me sit on his lap and take a picture?" Becka gave her sister a scandalous wink.

"You are out of your mind. I think college life is warping you" Nora reddened at the thought of the sexy Santa. Then she giggled.

"That is so wrong."

"Uh-oh," Becka grimaced. But her face beamed with unadulterated fascination. "This next group brought their dogs!"

Nora saw it too. "We'd better go before this gets ugly."

"But that's my favorite part," Becka protested as Nora dragged her away.

"You're terrible."

"Oh, we have to think up something for Jennifer Sharper's engagement party, too," Becka said suddenly as they walked away. "I guess she's getting married in January, and they're having a big affair at her dad's house." She shivered in excitement. "I can't wait!"

"I thought you didn't even like Jennifer that much."

"I like her well enough to go eat, drink and dance in her honor," Becka replied with a grin.

"Her dream come true, I'm sure," Nora replied dryly. "Thanks for inviting yourself, by the way."

Becka waved her off and led the way into a small boutique so quickly that Nora didn't get a glimpse of the name. All it sold were bags, big ugly leather ones that were obviously meant to be chic, or so the crisp black-and-white décor was meant to convince you. Some of the bags were large enough to fit a small child, but Nora couldn't see herself spending six hundred dollars on a glorified duffle bag. She was more of a shoe girl.

"It's not like you were going to bring a date to the engagement," Becka told her as she picked up and examined a slightly-less-ginoumous shoulder bag from its display. "I'm saving you from showing up alone."

Nora wished she had an argument to that, but Becka was frustratingly right. She'd been flirting with a fellow at her office, but it turned out he'd just been acting like a good co-worker. He was married, and Nora was the one who'd been reading too much into it. She sighed. *If you're married, you should wear your wedding ring.* Who cared if it was the twenty-first century? It was a courtesy to everyone else to just take yourself off the market and not give any lonely lawyers false hopes.

Annoyed, Nora took the bag from Becka's hands and put it back. "If you want to buy something to carry your entire course load of books in, I can get you one of those roller bags." Becka rolled her eyes, but chuckled and followed Nora out of the store.

They made their way along the row of shops, taking in the holiday decorations. The Christmas lights were up inside Northtown, strung along the balcony of the second level and wrapping around the banisters of the staircases. Christmas trees stood at intervals, glittering with tinsel, and big LED-lit stars hung along the ceiling high overhead.

Christmas was in the air, and Nora was

trying not to think too heavily on the emptiness of her condo when she went home in the evening. She was an adult for goodness' sake. She didn't need someone with her all the time, checking up on her, sending her texts to see if the firm had kept her working late. She didn't need somebody surprising her with dinner or sending her flowers at work.

And she certainly didn't need someone surprising her with coffee partway through her workday, when the paperwork got so tedious she wanted to curl up in a ball under her desk. Nope, she was fine. It was enough to have her family, to have a good job and a comfortable life. That was enough.

All those other things? The Hallmark love story moments; Nora didn't need them.

And if she could keep herself from thinking too hard about it, she could convince herself that she didn't want them either.

Chapter 10.

Laughing and joking with kids all day definitely wasn't what Colin was used to, but it had grown on him after a single hour at the Santa meet-and-greet. He'd been a little nervous when he showed up and asked to speak to 'the Santa people'. The phrase had slipped out, unintended, and Colin had been painfully aware of how insane he sounded.

But the lady in the mall office had understood, and within a half hour Colin was dressed up in the suit, padded as much as possible to make him slightly less lean. He still made a bit of a ripped Santa Claus, but so far, none of the mothers had complained. With the beard, the wig, and a bit of white make-up over his eyebrows, Colin could make it work.

Sure, there was the occasional parent who underestimated how frightened their child was of strangers. Some that still tried to get a picture taken of the poor kid, regardless. In fact, the amused, laughing father who was standing behind the photographer right now was probably finding his two-year-old's desperate struggle to roll off Colin's lap mighty entertaining. This picture would most likely come out of the woodworks in another sixteen years when graduation came around.

The boy's mother was not as entertained, however, and fretfully collected her toddler from Colin once the photograph was snapped. Colin quietly apologized for everything he could think of and then for his very existence as a Santa impersonator as the woman hurried her child back to his stroller.

"Well that was fun," the girl elf at his left muttered. She looked fifteen. Supposedly, you had to be eighteen or older to work at this display, or so Colin had been told by the manager. Given his own slapdash employment here, he got the feeling they weren't sticklers for the rules.

"Fun for you maybe," he muttered back. "All you have to do is smile and act drunk."

The supposedly eighteen-year-old chuckled. "Who says I'm acting?"

"You better be acting. I'm making a list. *And checking it twice.*"

The other elf was talking to the next family, trying to settle down the children in line. Unlike some of the other employees, she acted like she'd met a child at some point in her life, talking to them with reassurance and engaging them to help make the situation less intimidating.

A couple with a screaming child was walking away, obviously in the midst of a heating argument.

Colin murmured to his elf, "She looked like she was about to deck his halls." The elf rolled her eyes and snickered while Colin suppressed a laugh at the stupidity of his Santa-humor. The effect made him jiggle properly like the jolly fat man he was suppose to be. He put on a smile and pushed up the fake glasses he'd been given as the next child approached, this one blessedly happier.

"Oh, great," the elf sighed. "There's a whole busload of kids coming. An youth group or something. They're with a couple teachers and some church moms."

But Colin didn't get a chance to look up. He was in his Santa mode as the next little girl wandered up and introduced herself shyly.

In fact, Colin got no more than a hazy glimpse at the group of waiting kids. For one thing, there were intense lights pointed at him to help the photographer capture sellable pictures. And beyond literally not being able to see them well, he was also engrossed in character. It wasn't until the first child from the large group paused like a frightened deer six feet from Colin's chair that he got a look at the chaperones.

Colin felt the blood drain from his face as the beautiful woman from the coffee shop—the same one who'd been with the group of kids he'd seen out in the parking lot on Black Friday—stepped up to take the boy's hand.

"Come on, Luke," she said gently. "Don't be scared. He's nice, I promise." She smiled up at him, twinkling her eyes in a silent adult conspiracy. Colin thought he must have swallowed his tongue. She was in a baby blue cashmere sweater top this time, with her hair pulled into her signature bun.

The woman managed to coax the boy, who was maybe five or six, up to where Colin sat, sweating through the Santa suit. All he could think was that she was way too close. Surely, this close she'd recognize him. Surely.

Clinging to normalcy, Colin launched into his Santa act and managed to forget the lovely woman beside him. He and Luke had a friendly conversation about the Boys and Girls Club, whose logo was emblazoned on the little boys shirt. However, when Colin glanced back up, she was looking at him intently.

At that moment, the photographer asked her to step out of the picture for a moment, and she obliged quickly, stepping over to join the group of waiting kids. Colin thought that maybe she was still trying to get a good look at him, even from twelve feet off.

The next few kids were not nearly so afraid, and there proved to be no need for her to approach again. Colin was more than a little thankful for that. The last thing he needed was for the cute Starbucks lady to think he worked full-time as a mall Santa.

— —

It wasn't until later, when he was working on the engagement gift he'd been commissioned to create, that Colin realized that the woman in the neatly pressed suit at Starbucks was quite different than the friendly, mothering woman in the soft sweaters. Maybe even different enough to take a second look at an unemployed welder.

Nah, he decided, and dropped his face mask back in place.

Chapter 11.

Jennifer Sharper hadn't been the sweetest girl when the two of them had gone to high school together. Nora recalled many unfavorable memories with Jennifer, although they'd lingered in the same general friend circle for the four years before graduation. Their parents, however, had been in the same social circles for much of their lives, hence her inclusion on the invite list.

The house that Nora and Becka pulled up

to looked more like a country club than a private residence. A valet took their car, sparing them a walk from the parking area through the gathering snowdrifts.

"Not bad," Becka muttered.

The front foyer was like walking into the White House. A grand double staircase wound up two opposite walls, leading to rooms on the upper floors. Hundreds of soft yellow lights were strung up for the holidays, casting the entire interior of the house in an otherworldly glow. It all looked so pristine, as if this wasn't the house where the Sharper's lives really took place.

Nora and Becka had dressed as the invitation told them, Black Tie Optional. Both girls were in evening dresses as were most of the other female attendees. Becka's A-line was navy blue with a light shimmer, while Nora wore a graceful sheath in pure black offset with a gorgeous chunky statement bracelet and draping earrings. The elegant black dress had a slit leading up one side—higher than she would have preferred normally, but her tempestuous sister insisted her legs were long enough to get away with it. There wasn't a man in sight who wasn't in a suit, most with ties, but a few rising to the occasion in a proper tux. Everyone had drinks in hand, so after the hosts of the party greeted the girls, they set off in pursuit of their own. Nora hardly recognized Jennifer, who fluttered by without recognition. She had obviously dieted within an inch of her life for the occasion.

There was a live band playing gentle jazzy background music, and a ballroom with an enormous wall of windows looking out into an ethereal, snow-frosted garden under strings of outdoor fairy lights. Nora was spellbound. A moment later she was jostled back to consciousness when Becka caught sight of the bar and pulled Nora over.

"What'll it be?"

"An Old Fashioned and a vodka cranberry, please," Becka told him without asking Nora. Over the last few years, they'd gone to an event or two together, and Becka knew what Nora always ordered. She liked her Old Fashioneds.

With a few shakes of the sleek metal cocktail shaker, two glasses were poured and pushed across the bar with precision execution. Nora thanked the clean-shaven bartender as she picked up her Waterford glass. She took a sip off the top of the tea brown drink and pushed the cherry to the bottom. Becka followed Nora as she slowly weaved through the crowd.

"This is cool," Becka whispered loudly. Nora had to agree that the swanky soiree was pretty impressive. They made their way through the crowd, doing a circle of the main room.

The two of them were running into a blockage at the edge of the ballroom. Some sort of crowd had clogged up the edge of the dance floor, ogling something. Nora could see barely something metallic gleaming near the back wall.

"It's like an exhibit or something," she told Becka, who was definitely the shorter sister.

"Well, cool. Let's look closer."

And then Becka began gently elbowing her way through the crowd, proving that although Nora was the tall sister, Becka was the bossy one.

"Oh, my," Nora gasped.

The art that everyone was captured by was a glorious wall-size landscape, made entirely of metal. The sheets were all in burnished bronze and coppery shades, practically shimmering in the warm light. It depicted a mountain rising over a serene metal lake, surrounded by metal pine trees. A welded elk nosed peacefully, a tiny shape in the shadow of the rising mountain. A full moon peered over the mountain's shoulder, wrought in some metal that shone pale gold.

Becka was saying something, but Nora was staring, bewitched.

"Nora!"

Nora shook her head and looked down at her sister.

"I guess this is an engagement gift," Becka told her. "Someone from the groom's side had it made from some local artist. It's really nice."

That was an understatement. The metal landscape was impossible to look away from. It was hypnotizing. No wonder a crowd was standing around it, silent with awe.

Becka moved on after some cute man in a suit. With a chuckle, Nora let her go. Her eyes were glued to the piece. It was so… elegantly simple and expressive. Nora wasn't a fine art buff, and she didn't know a thing about metalworking. All she knew is that it ignited a feeling in her chest, a fascinating contentment. Transcendent, like the moonrise.

After a long while, Nora moved back and let someone else get close enough for a good look. She'd been impressed by the house and the atmosphere. But that art was something different.

She turned to go look for Becka and nearly bowled right over one of her fellow guests. The remains of her old fashioned splashed over his suit jacket.

"I'm so sorry!" she cried. Nora swiped at his jacket. "I am *so* sorry!"

"It's fine," he said, waving her off. "Don't even worry about it. I stole this jacket off some guy in the parking lot."

Nora looked up and saw the humor in his eye. She relaxed and tried to smile. He smiled back, and suddenly, the memory clicked into place.

"Hey! I saw you at Starbucks once!"

He chuckled nervously and nodded. "Yeah. The doors here didn't give you any trouble, did they? I wasn't there to... you know... hold it..."

He laughed and pinned his lips shut. Nora let a giggle escape. "No, no trouble tonight. I guess the door saw you come in and it was too afraid to give me any grief."

She tried not to be too obvious as she looked him up and down. He'd been wearing jeans and a flannel coat when they met at Starbucks. She'd noticed his dirty blond hair and handsome face, but now she could see the rest of him matched perfectly. Broad shoulders held up the suit jacket. His tapered frame was visible as his crisp white shirt, which he wore unbuttoned to the collarbone, followed the V shape. The dress slacks bulged over muscular thighs. He wore a deep purple pocket square that complimented his green eyes.

"Nora," she said, extending her hand.

"Colin," he replied. He shook her hand and then, as if he'd had to think about it, he lifted her knuckles to his lips in a brief kiss. She thought she saw a quick flush pass over his cheeks with the gesture.

"So," Nora said quickly, afraid he might run off. "Are you here with the bride, or the groom?"

It seemed like a straightforward question, but he thought about it longer than she expected. Finally he chuckled and shrugged. "The groom, I guess. Sort of both."

Sort of both? Nora didn't know what to make of that, but he didn't explain further. "I'm with the bride, but I have to admit, I'm not sure how I earned an invitation." Conspiratorially, Nora leaned in to whisper. "We haven't spoken in years. Social obligation, I imagine."

Colin laughed. "I was surprised to get an

invite, myself. But it looks like a lot of these people were pulled from all over the place. I'm not even sure I know this many people on a first name basis."

Nora looked around and examined her fellow guests. They were all dressed to the nines. Evening dresses and suits and flawless make-up.

"I'm pretty sure I don't, either," Nora admitted. She looked down at her empty glass and smiled. "Want to come get a drink with me?"

Colin agreed with a smile, and they threaded back through the crowded ballroom to the lounge with the open bar. When they squeezed in, Colin tried to wave the bartender down.

At that moment, Nora saw Becka headed her way, looking at the tall stranger with interest. Frantically, Nora waved her away. Becka gave her a devious grin, and Nora motioned for her to make herself scarce. With a silent snicker, Becka gave Nora the gesture for *I'm watching you,* but thankfully relented and headed back into the crowd.

Nora turned back to see the man behind the bar waiting, and Colin watching her with a raised eyebrow.

"Oh, an old fashioned, please," Nora told the bartender sweetly.

With a glass apiece, Nora and Colin found an empty table and sat down to talk.

"Did you see that landscape?" Nora asked him, remembering suddenly. She'd nearly spilled her drink on him not twenty feet from the artwork, but he might not have gotten the chance to see.

His grin turned secretive. "You mean the engagement gift? Yeah, I saw it."

"I've never seen anything like it," Nora gushed. The drink was helping, but she'd figured out that Colin was a little shy, but she got the feeling that he was someone who opened up once he had warmed up to you. He was handsome enough that the effort was worth it.

"Really?" he asked. His secretive smile opened in excitement. "It's a… a really unique gift, I guess."

"I'll say," Nora agreed. "I forgot to ask who the artist is. Someone local, I think."

"The artist's name isn't on it," Colin told her. "It's a secret."

Nora laughed. "We have a secret artist on the loose."

Colin took a sip of his drink and sighed. "Time to make up the wanted posters."

His hands had caught Nora's eye at the bar, and she looked at them closely, now. They were big, which matched the rest of him, from his broad shoulders to his towering height. The nails were short and uneven, and if she wasn't mistaken, still with a bit of dirt under them.

Slyly, she looked back up at his face. "So what do you do?"

"I'm a welder," he admitted with a shrug. Just then an upbeat holiday song began playing, causing the dance floor to populate.

"Do welders dance?" she cautioned, feeling bold with her second drink and the warmth of their close bodies.

"Welders have been known to a cut a rug or two," Colin returned. He almost followed that up with a relatively lame carpenter joke, but thankfully stopped himself.

Colin stood, tipped back the remainder of his glass and offered her his hand. "Shall we?"

Nora wasn't a huge dancer at parties, but she loved to just cut loose and have fun when she was with the right people. There were so many people at the engagement party that it was easy to feel hidden in plain sight, leaving them free to dance without anyone paying much attention.

They danced for the next five songs, which fluctuated between up-tempo dance numbers and medium paced ones where Colin twirled her around and they made up the moves as they went. Nora's smile felt huge across her face as she was twirled and swirled under his arm and around the dance floor. They made funny conversation between songs and several times as they danced. After the band's rendition of *It's The Most Wonderful Time of the Year* came to an end, Colin dipped her deeply in a melodramatic move. When he pulled her up, a slow, romantic song began to swell up and around him. Still breathing hard from giggling, Nora found a comforting relief as Colin pulled her to him, there hands intertwined, her face resting gently in the sway underneath his shoulder. She could feel the top of her head brush lightly against his jaw. He smelled like Christmas pine and cinnamon, and the dance was a slow, swaying dream. When the final notes hit, they lingered for a minute before pulling back to look at one another.

"Do you want to go outside for a little fresh air?" Colin suggested.

Nora nodded agreeably. That was exactly what she wanted to do. He took her hand in his, and lead her through the crowd. This must be what it's like to have a bodyguard, she thought to her own amusement. As the crowd was thick, she had a few minutes to savor the strength of his hand, gently covering hers. She could feel the thickness of where he must hold his tools. These were definitely not hands used for punching computer keys or flipping through long legal documents. For a fleeting second, she thought of what it would feel like I he were to slip his hand around her bare back and pull her close. The image flustered her and she had to shake it from her mind. She needed that cold outdoor air stat! Colin pushed the door open and Nora entered into the enchanted courtyard. It felt like a scene out of a movie, a regal winter wonderland. Nora began to walk toward some seating placed next to a roaring outdoor fireplace, when suddenly a shrill voice cut through the air. "Nora! There you are! I haven't seen you in forever!"

It was Jennifer Sharper, of course, and Nora tried to smile as she turned and accepted the half-drunk hug from the blonde bride-to-be. A gaggle of high-heeled and unsteady woman had followed behind Jennifer, and it was clear that they were heading back inside, and now meant to take Nora with them. She looked over her shoulder at Colin in dismay as she was flocked away.

"Don't worry," Jennifer told him with exaggerated certainty. "We'll bring her right back."

That was a lie. It was time for the party to really begin, and a slew of wedding-themed games and dances were in full swing in the ballroom. Nora was dragged into it, and didn't have the heart to excuse herself and try to track down her handsome welder again.

By the time she and Becka was staggering towards the door at the end of the night, half of the party guests were asleep in chairs or muttering to each other over mostly-empty bottles of champagne. If it weren't November, dawn would be approaching; the clock on the dash in Nora's car read four forty-nine as she eased out of the parking area and found her way back into Evanswood.

"Let me know if Jenny invites you to any more parties," Becka murmured sleepily, leaning against the window.

Nora didn't answer. Colin had disappeared after Jennifer dragged her away, and with the way he looked tonight, Nora was convinced that she could have found him again if he'd stayed at the party. She sighed in disappointment. Another few minutes, and she would have asked for his number. Now, she didn't even know his last name, and unless she found a way to talk to Jennifer Sharper again, there was no way to find out. It had been made known last night that Jennifer, her fiancé and her family, were to be on a plane first thing in the morning to celebrate Christmas in Zurich. Finding out the name of a random Prince Charming probably didn't count as emergency enough to go through the rigmarole of tracking down the Sharper clan.

Colin hadn't been wearing a wedding ring. Nora had looked at his hands long enough to be sure of that. His hands looked worn and rough, but strong, and Nora shivered to imagine what sorts of things they were capable of. No wedding ring...

Of course, it was the twenty-first century,

and some people just didn't wear wedding bands. Nora fervently hoped that Colin wasn't among them.

Chapter 12.

"Colin? You out here?"

He could hardly hear over the hiss of the torch in his hand. Colin looked up to see his sister Carol in the doorway of his workshop. He cut the heat on his welding torch and flipped his eye protector up. The weather was seasonally cold, with a week left until Christmas, but he was still sweating in his coveralls, gloves, and face shield. He swiped an arm across his forehead.

"Hey! What's up?"

Carol jabbed a thumb towards the house. "I just brought some leftovers over. Dad thinks you're going to starve to death."

Colin rolled his eyes. "I know how to cook."

"You know how to use a microwave." Carol came closer to look at the sculpture he was working on. It wasn't his sturgeon leaping from the water this time. His sister tugged her scarf a little looser; his workshop was fairly toasty with all the welding. "Is this a new commission?"

The shape was becoming clear; it was an ornate metal cross, delicately scaled in a thousand tiny pieces of scrap metal to create an almost effervescent effect. Colin nodded.

"Yeah. Your church asked me to make it, actually. St. Joseph's. They want to auction it off as part of some partnership with the Heart Association's annual charity fundraiser.

Obviously, I couldn't say no to that."

"Wow." Carol examined the intricate metal bands. Even half-done, Colin could still tell she found it impressive. He rarely saw his sister impressed. These days, she was usually running after her brood of offspring, or yelling at the dogs. A spear of guilt hit him in the gut. Maybe he should take her out to a movie or something. He'd let Carol take care of their dad, take care of everything after their mom passed away. If she was exhausted and overworked, he felt that at least part of it was his fault.

"Is Andrew working tonight?"

Carol nodded. "He picked up all the overtime he could so that we can afford for him to take some time off."

With a yawn, Colin looked at his watch and realized he'd been out here for six hours. The time had flown.

Carol leaned against his worktable and

crossed her arms. "I meant to ask, how'd that party go? Did they like that sculpture you made?"

"They loved it," Colin answered, leaning against the table next to her. "That's actually how St. Joseph's got a hold of me. I guess someone at the party goes to their church, and they asked Andrew's friend who made it."

"Through the grapevine," Carol agreed, smiling. "Well, I'm glad you're making some money from this. I think you like it a lot." That last part was a sisterly intuition. Colin chuckled, thinking of Nora.

"I think I do, too," he said. "It was really nice, having people admire my work. But I think it'll be better when I get a welding job again."

Carol looked at him in surprise. "Really? Why?"

"You know why," he said. "The same reason why Mom never stopped working to write full-time. It's just not steady enough, you know? I mean, I'm doing this piece as a donation."

With a sigh, Carol wrapped an arm around his waist. "But Mom also never got to finish her book, don't forget. Everything she wrote, we printed out and put in a binder... just to keep..." Carol coughed, and Colin put his arm around her shoulders. Carol pushed on, her voice a little hoarse. "We'll never know how she meant to end it, because she would never spend the time on it."

Colin put his other arm around his sister and kissed the top of her head. "She wanted to spend her time with us."

Carol nodded and wiped at her eyes. "I know. I just... all those half-written pages really get to me, you know? I go and I look through them sometimes, and I—I just wish she'd gotten to—to finish it."

His eyes were welling up with tears now

too, and Colin swallowed a lump in his throat. "Come on, Carol. I'm not Mom. I'm not going anywhere anytime soon."

Carol laughed through her tears. "Of course you aren't. You have award-winning sculptures to create."

Relieved that their conversation was taking a light tack, Colin laughed. "Exactly. And don't you worry about me starving; the Denny's up the road has a table with my name on it."

Carol shoved him playfully.

"Oh hey! This is kinda just an experiment, but I wanted to show you something." Colin walked over to a small box sitting on his workbench. He grabbed a polishing rag and creaked open the box. As Carol came over to see, Colin took the delicate ring out of it's resting place and ran the cloth around it.

"Here, see if it fits." Colin handed the ring to Carol, whose mouth was agape. She took the smooth metal ring between her fingers and held it up to the light. Tiny detailed etchings were intricately woven onto the surface, leading up to and encircling a gleaming aquamarine stone.

"Colin, this is-" Carol continued to take in the ring, still unable to wrap her head around her brother having made something so small and beautiful.

"It's your birthstone. Like I said, it was just an experiment," he looked a little bashful about it and shrugged. "I was going to give it to you for Christmas, for always taking such good care of me. But, I don't know. Tonight seems good too."

"Colin, I...this is the most beautiful ring I've ever seen." She slipped it on her finger and inspected it. "I can't believe you made this. Can I keep it?"

Colin laughed, "Yeah, of course. I mean, it's not an everyday ring, it was just something I wanted to try and I thought who better to make it for." He smiled at his sister who still couldn't break her gaze from the ring adorning her finger.

"I guess I better call it a night," Colin sighed. He unplugged the torch and doubled-checked that everything was cooling. "I forget to eat, I forget to sleep. It's a wonder I've made it this far."

Carol opened his workshop door and they walked out into the falling snow. "I already have three kids. Don't add yourself to the list of people I have to watch over twenty-four seven."

The night was serene, a glowing mid-December night. Colin didn't have Christmas lights on his house, but his neighbors did, and a shimmering tinsel tree hung from the streetlight. A light snow was falling, looking like flakes of gold as it drifted through the yellow lamplight, settling on the road in a thick blanket.

"You better head home. It's getting too deep for your car, and the plows don't come through my street first."

Carol agreed, and leaned up to give her brother a hug and a kiss on the cheek. "Thank you for this." She wiggled her fingers in the air, showing off her new jewelry. "I left the food in your fridge. It's probably not too cold yet, if you eat it now."

She climbed into her car. "Oh! Hey Colin, have you called Frank & Sons yet?"

Guiltily, Colin shrunk into his big shoulders. "No."

Carol glared over the frame of her car door. "Good." She cracked a sisterly smile, "I think something better is just around the corner."

His looked up at her surprised and Carol shut the car door. Her reverse lights flared, and she backed out onto the street. Colin watched until she was out of sight, and then retreated out of the cold, back into his house.

He found the leftovers she'd brought: pot roast with boiled vegetables. Colin put the whole thing in the microwave eagerly. He hadn't eaten since the morning and home cooked food was exactly what he needed.

Chapter 13.

The Monday before Christmas, Nora was at the Northtown Mall again. The only person left to shop for was Becka; Nora was beginning to think that it would be much easier to just buy her sister a gift card. Nora loved her sister, but it was hard to buy a gift for someone who rarely waited to be given what they wanted.

Outside Macy's, Nora stopped and leaned on the rail, looking around at the shoppers on every side. A lot of people saw Becka as selfish. There were times when Nora agreed. But at least her little sister never had to wonder if she'd ever get the things she needed in her life. If there was ever a change to make or a chance to pursue, Becka just did it, and got things done.

Nora had always tended to take the long way around. The scenic route always held surprises, things you didn't even think of. Law school had been a slow, steady progress, taking challenges one at a time, and never rushing faster than her comfort zone wanted to allow. And because of that, Nora had a comfortable life. Up until now, she'd thought this was the life she wanted.

But maybe Becka was onto something, because Nora knew that if it had been her sitting at that table with Colin the other night, Becka would have gotten more than his number. Nora had played it safe again, trying to take the long way around, and before she knew it she was hijacked off to dance the Macarena and play engagement bingo with people she barely knew. All while missing the chance to spend time with someone that she wanted to know better.

Of course, Nora reminded herself, he was probably married. Good looking, with a good job, and an adorable shy smile. He was definitely married, he had to be. But now Nora would never know.

With a sigh, she turned and thought about going through Macy's. Even from here, she could see it was a madhouse inside. The line at the cash register was a quarter mile long, and the displays were a frantic mess. Sometimes Nora stumbled across pretty outfits in Macy's. But unless they'd decided to open a department dedicated to shopping for impulsive younger sisters, there really wasn't a good reason to go there today.

Nora walked away from Macy's and wandered down the line of smaller stores. She passed the oversized bag boutique, but even though she loved her sister, she couldn't bring herself to do it. But when she was past the boutique, another thought came to mind. There was a store on the other side of the mall that was perfect, she thought excitedly.

Excited, now, Nora scanned over the mall directory and mapped in her head which way to go.

On the way, Nora passed by the Santa meet-and-greet again. It looked like a different Santa on duty today, which was a shame. Becka had been right, after all. That other actor had been one hunky Santa.

Nora stopped again as a second revelation hit her. The madness of it was overwhelming. She looked at the Santa in the red and gold chair; it definitely wasn't the same guy, because she knew, now, what he looked like under the hair and beard.

She inched closer to the elf lingering near the fence; there were three today, as if the keep up with the staggering line of waiting families.

"Excuse me?" she said hesitantly.

The elf looked over. She had to still be in high school. "Hello! Merry Christmas, ma'am, what can I do for you?"

"Hey, do you know the other Santa that works here?" Nora asked.

The girl looked at her suspiciously. Nora felt strange for someone in fake ears and jingle-bell shoes to be giving her the side eye. "We aren't supposed to give out personal information... Why?"

Nora bit back the excitement of discovery. "His name is Colin, right?"

The elf nodded again. "Well, yeah. What about him?"

"Do you know his last name?"

The girl looked over at her co-workers; it

was hard to tell if she was silently asking for help or checking to see if anyone was looking. It looked as though the two of them were unobserved, so she turned back to Nora.

"It's MacCullough," she admitted. "Colin MacCullough."

"Sounds very Irish."

"He *looks* pretty Irish."

"Is he…" Nora chewed her lip, trying to frame her question. "Is he… into men?"

That was not the question the girl was expecting. She gave a sudden snort of laughter. "I doubt it." She snickered again as if the possibility still amused her.

Nora wasn't really sure whether she wanted to know the answer to her next question. But she was channeling her impulsive, grab-life-by-the-collar sister, and she figured that she might as well ask. "Do you know if he's married? Or with anyone?"

She held her breath while the elf girl

thought about it. Finally, the girl twisted her mouth in a frown. "You know... I don't think so. He doesn't flirt back with me, but I think he thinks I'm in high school."

Nora was tempted to ask if the girl was in high school, but she was too eager to move on. She thanked the elf helper and waved goodbye.

There was just a little bit of shopping left to do, and then it was time to see if she could track down Colin MacCullough.

Chapter 14.

At St. Joseph's Church, Colin was lingering in a tiny annex room with the finished project that he'd delivered. Tonight was the night it was suppose to be auctioned off for charity. It had turned out beautifully, but Colin was still nervous.

For the moment, he was alone with his thoughts, for which Colin was thankful. He'd taken a job to make something, and it had turned out well. Then he'd been contacted to make something else, and it had turned out good. In a strange way, it felt as if his life was shifting around him. Maybe his luck had changed?

Luck, or Carol's words. No one was more surprised than Colin when he actually decided not to call Frank & Sons the day after talking to Carol in the garage. Something about the world of white snow and freshness of air, or maybe the feeling of Christmas approaching, less than a week away, had settled in his chest. And Colin had made the decision that he wasn't going back to his old life. He could always get a welding job. He was skilled, and a hard worker. There would always be something out there for him. But what he wasn't sure of was whether he would always have the opportunities that he suddenly found himself with. The last few days had fielded phone calls about other commissions, metal sculptures and even some jewelry pieces. It seemed that Carol had been flashing her new ring around and people had taken notice.

Colin sighed and ran a hand over the metal-worked cross. He was proud he'd been entrusted to make something that would do some good in the world. The idea of it was pretty powerful. His simple act of plying metal into something he thought was beautiful would possibly be bought by someone who actually wanted to display the thing that *he* made in their home. And the money they spent would go directly to help families dealing with overwhelming medical needs. The nervousness in his heart reared up again. He hoped someone bought it.

Maybe he was an artist after all. He crinkled his nose and laughed to himself at the idea. He may have to get use to that a bit more before he said it out loud.

"Mr. MacCullough?"

One of the auction staff came in, followed

by two church volunteers to move the auction piece up into the viewing area for the guests to take a close look at before the bidding began. Colin lent a hand moving the piece, as he knew how heavy and awkward it was.

Up in the gallery, a circle of art pieces waited for the auction to start. There was an obvious open display stand for the cross, and Colin let the other two volunteers steer in the direction. They managed to get the sculpture on the stand without incident, where it rested placidly, catching the spotlights and sitting in a halo of reflected brilliance.

A group of admirers flocked to it at once, and Colin backed away quickly. He straightened his suit jacket and quietly allowed the audience to ogle his work. He'd carried it in with the other volunteers, so no one seemed to credit him with it.

"This one's nice."

Colin jumped. There she was again, Nora,

the woman from Starbucks, the one from the mall, the one from the engagement party. She just kept popping up, and it was hard to tell whether this was good or bad thing.

Tonight, her straight hair was in a shimmering sheet down around her shoulders, and she was wearing a lovely green sweater-dress that was modest enough for a church, but just clingy enough to make an imaginative man wonder. For all intents and purposes, Colin chalked this meeting up to the 'good' column.

And right now, she was admiring his art. He tried to look casual, which was difficult when he was nervous. Colin didn't like to play poker for exactly this reason.

"I was wondering what this piece was going to be," Nora commented casually. "I heard it's by the same artist as the one at the engagement party."

Colin looked at her out of the corner of his

eye. Was she hinting? He felt himself start to sweat, an irrational reaction, but a powerful one all the same.

"Do you go to this church?" he asked.

She leaned closer. "No. I'm actually on the Heart Association Fundraising Committee. But we were running short on volunteers so I said I would help with guarding the doors during the actual auction."

"So you're guarding the doors in case anyone tried to make a mad dash with any of the auction items, eh?" he chuckled.

"Oh, don't be deceived; I'm much bigger than I look. There will be no thefts tonight. Not through my door." she replied impishly.

"So are you bidding tonight?"

"Me?" he laughed. "I'm a welder. I don't make enough money to bid in these things."

"You did say that," Nora nodded. "Would I have heard of where you work?"

Not sure how to answer, he shoved his

hands in his suit pockets. "I doubt it. But I'm currently getting to enjoy the holidays, so not too much focus on working."

"That's good. I hear Christmas is Santa's busiest night of the year."

At first, her comment didn't make a bit of sense. Colin was watching the crowd around his art, and puzzled for a minute about what on Earth she meant.

And then, like a brick, it hit him. Colin's entire body froze, and he looked down at Nora to see she was smiling like a cat with a mouse. The blood rushed to his face, and he felt his cheeks reddening wildly.

"If everyone could please take their seats, now." A prim, stern-faced woman appeared at the open door of the large room where the auction was being held. "We're ready to begin the auction, ladies and gentleman."

Another staffer appeared at his elbow. "Mr. MacCullough, if you could come with me," she said kindly, nodding at Nora.

Colin had never been so happy to escape in his life. With a red-faced nod, he fled, following after the woman as she led him inside.

Chapter 15.

Nora stood in the back of the hall with the other volunteer who was attending the door. She'd been so excited to see Colin again! Was the entire world determined to interrupt?

She tried to spot him in the audience, but he wasn't sitting among the guests. He'd said that he wasn't bidding, tonight, so Nora wasn't expecting to find him there anyway. With his height, even if he'd been in the seats, she would have seen him.

To her surprise, Nora saw Colin sooner than expected. When the metalwork cross came up for bidding, it was introduced as belonging to him, crafted in full by Mr. Colin MacCullough.

Standing there in the spotlight next to his sculpture, he'd never looked so handsome, or so shy. His suit fit him just as perfectly and Nora could swear that every woman in the room let out a collective, admiring sigh.

But Nora could hardly believe her eyes. Did this mean that he'd made the landscape, too? He'd said that he was a welder. Where did a blue-collar worker learn to make such stunning art?

Looking at him now, Nora suspected that if she tried to ask him, he'd be too embarrassed to answer.

She couldn't help but grin. He was too much. Built like a college football player, and as sweet as a seventh-grade boy.

The bidding started for his artwork, but Nora's attention was fixed on him. She saw his every expression, and when his sculpture was auctioned away for $50,000, she thought she could tell he was barely able to keep his own jaw from dropping.

As the piece was wheeled off the stage, Colin was escorted off as well. She saw him gracefully slip into the shadows and from the look he gave her when she outed him as Santa, she imagined he was about to make a hasty exit.

She turned to her fellow volunteer. "Do you think you could watch the door?"

The woman smiled and winked. "Yep. Go get him."

Nora felt herself redden, though not as badly as Colin did. "You saw him leave, too?"

The other volunteer, an older mom who Nora knew for a fact had been happily married for over twenty years, fanned herself theatrically. "Everybody saw him leave honey, believe me."

Hesitant, Nora grimaced. "I hate to leave just for that."

The woman waved her through the meeting room door. "Let me put it to you this way: I can't chase him myself, but I'm not getting in the way of you finding a guy like that under *your* Christmas tree. Go catch that man!"

Nora intended to do just that, and left with a hasty thank-you. He wasn't in the hall when she left the meeting room, and he wasn't in the entryway of the church. She grabbed her coat and hurried carefully out into the icy parking lot, but she didn't see anyone's car running.

And then she realized—if he'd brought in his artwork, he'd probably parked in the back!

Nora got there too late. His taillights were swinging out of the church parking lot by the time she managed to navigate the snow walkway to the rear of St. Joseph's. And once again, Nora found herself standing there wondering: *Why do I always go the long way?*

Chapter 16.

It was Christmas Eve, and the Starbucks was closing down until December 26th.

Colin sat in an empty chair by the door, waiting for his coffee. Considering it was Christmas Eve, the place was pretty busy. A group of high school Christmas carolers were parked in the center of the place, laughing and singing snippets of songs. It seemed they'd already been out around the neighborhood for the few hours of dusk and evening. There was a decidedly cheery, festive feeling in the little coffee shop, and Colin was in no rush to leave.

A little over a month ago he'd sat in this same seat, in almost the same clothes, and brooded over losing what he thought was his livelihood. At the time, he never would have guessed at the odd turns his life was going to take, and the bizarre chances he'd be thrown. He certainly never expected to be working in a Santa outfit.

Colin leaned his head back with a smile. He was going to Carol's house next. They'd watch *Jingle All the Way* and have a nice fire. They'd listen to Christmas music and tell the kids that if they didn't go to sleep quick, Santa was going to pass over the house.

In fact, Colin had even tried to borrow the Santa outfit from the mall. It turned out he wasn't allowed to take it home, but Carol had assured him that if anyone showed up to the house in costume, the overexcited children and animals would tear the whole place down.

In about two weeks, he was going to start on the next phase of his life, and Colin was happy with that. He had taken a residency at the prestigious Art Museum, where they wanted him to basically work on new pieces all day long for the next few months. They would supply the workshop, any tools he needed, as well as a pretty decent stipend. He also had several more commissions lined up for both sculptural pieces, as well as some jewelry pieces that he was really excited to work out. Between the residency and the high-end clientele that seemed to passing his name around, he had the sense that his work was going to have some good exposure in the upcoming year. He found absolute peace with leaving the life of supervised manual labor behind. He was free to make whatever life he wanted for himself, and every day that he was away from the routine of his old life, he saw more and more opportunities unfold before him. He had spent years living and dreaming within the confines of what his peers thought of as achievable. Those things were good and fine, but Colin had started to see the world in color, through his own eyes. And things that he had never thought possible for himself suddenly seamed attainable. It was empowering in a way which he could never have imagined. He felt renewed and excited about life. He felt truly blessed; with many new beginnings just around the corner.

Snow was falling calmly outside the big wall of windows. Colin watched it sleepily. He'd sleep over at Carol and Andrew's on the couch tonight, and wake up with children jumping on him in the morning. It was a fate he was resigned to. They would have breakfast and open presents, and Colin wouldn't worry about how he was going to make a living next year. The world, for just a fragile moment, was all in one piece, and he savored it.

His hot peppermint mocha was called out, and Colin got to his feet. The baristas were running to keep up with the orders coming in from both the store and the drive-thru. Just as he reached for his mocha, a standard cup of black coffee was set beside it and called out. A woman's gloved hand reached out to take it, and Colin found himself suddenly face-to-face with Nora.

"Oh." That was all that came out of his mouth. Colin coughed and tried again. "Hey! M-Merry Christmas."

"Merry Christmas!" Nora replied with a smile. She took his arm and led him away from the counter, where the next order was already steaming.

Colin stood there, holding his coffee. He took a sip, trying to put off the inevitable moment when he'd have to find something coherent to say to this woman that he'd developed an all-consuming crush on. Usually he felt fine talking to people, even beautiful women, but all their missed encounters, all the time he'd spent thinking about her had built up a total block of nerves.

"So," Nora started with a smile. "You're the mysterious artist, huh?"

Colin could already feel the heat in his face. "Yeah," he agreed.

Nora elbowed him. "And the Santa at Northtown."

His eyebrows rose sharply. Now he was definitely blushing. "Uh… yep."

"And a welder, too," Nora nodded. He dared a glance at her face; she was still smiling. That was a good sign. "A man of many talents."

"That's what I put on my business cards, anyway," Colin answered with a chuckle. Nora laughed.

"It's really warm in here, with coats and all," she said, indicating her thick peacoat and gloves. "Want to go outside?"

Colin did. Now that she had his heart pounding in his ears, some cool air would be a blessing. She was dressed sleek and elegant again, while he found himself looking just as rough and tumble as the first time he'd seen her. Even so, as they stood outside the door to Starbucks, Nora's eyes were on him, and he'd have to be completely dense to misunderstand her thoughts.

"So," she started slowly. "I wanted to ask how you'd feel about going out together sometime."

Had she just said that? Colin forced his mouth to start moving before he froze like a deer.

"Yeah, that would be great. I... I didn't know if you'd be interested."

Nora took out her phone, handling it

awkwardly in gloves and with one hand still on her coffee cup. "Now, I'm going to get your number this time. People keep interrupting before I can ask."

Colin gave it to her, hardly daring to believe this was happening. She sent him a text, and Colin heard the tone go off through his pocket. He had her phone number. And here he thought he didn't believe in Christmas miracles.

"Thanks." It sounded silly the moment he heard himself say it, but Nora didn't seem to mind. She giggled, and looked absolutely stunning there in the light from the window, with crystal snowflakes catching in her brown hair.

"Have you ever been to London?" she asked suddenly.

Colin stared, and shook his head. "Nope."

Nora smiled. "I haven't either, but I'm taking my sister next week, before she goes back to school. So if you call, and I don't answer, I might be asleep, because of the time difference. But don't think I ignored your call, because I'll be waiting to hear from you. And I have your number, too, now. I'd like to see you again, Colin."

To his surprise, Nora reached up and kissed him on the cheek. And Colin surprised himself—apparently he wasn't as shy around beautiful women as he thought, because he caught Nora's chin lightly and kissed her on the lips. Her eyes opened in surprise, but she didn't pull away.

When they separated Nora's cheeks were a little red, perhaps from more than cold. She murmured, teasing, "I never thought I'd relate to the song, *I Saw Mommy Kissing Santa Clause*, but I definitely get it now." She was half embarrassed that that had been her response, and half proud for being so quick and witty. Then she realized that she was in a complete daze, staring up at Colin's lips.

She blinked her eyes clear, then smiled up at him. This taking life by the reigns was fun already! Colin was smiling down at her, too. For some strange reason, she felt that if they both played their cards right, there could be many more holiday kisses in their future.

"If I didn't have to make this Christmas Eve delivery before going to my parents' house, I would say we should go for a walk, but..." Nora let out a sigh and shrugged her shoulders.

"That would be nice, but you're right, we should both get going. Walk you to your car?" he offered. Nora nodded; suppressing the giddy smile she felt bubbling up.

She got in the driver's seat and rolled down the window. Colin stood beside the car, holding his peppermint mocha, unintentionally giving her his most charming grin. She pulled out of the spot and then stopped for just one more moment. A question popped into her head, and however silly, she felt compelled to ask.

"Strange question. But do you believe in Christmas miracles?"

Colin's grin grew wider, then took a second before he shook his head subtly. "Before this month, if you'd asked me that, I don't know what I would have said. But right this moment? I can tell you that without a doubt, yes. Yes, I do." Their eyes couldn't break from one another.

"I'm going to call you tomorrow and wish you a merry Christmas, okay?"

Still awestruck, she just nodded, then managed out, "Okay."

Nora slowly moved her foot off the brake petal and the car eased forward. Her heart was fluttering a thousand beats a minute and her face felt flush. As she looked in her rear view mirror, she no longer saw Colin standing there, but through the air came the low, booming sound - *Ho, Ho, Ho*

Nora laughed out loud, then pressed the gas.

If you enjoyed this story, please consider leaving a Review on Amazon and/or Goodreads!

Every single review makes a tremendous difference. I cannot express how much I appreciate that you took the time to read this book. From the bottom of my heart, thank you.

~ Sophie & the Love Light Faith family

ACKNOWLEDGEMENT

Thank you to my wonderful family and friends. You make my world go 'round.

To Drake: Brainstorming with you is always the highlight of any evening. Thank you for being my partner in crime... even when you're overworked and overtired.

To my parents: Thank you for teaching me to always look ahead at what can be, instead of getting bogged down by the difficult things that life presents. I owe my silver-lining outlook and crisis management skills to you, and couldn't be more thankful.

To Emily: Thank you so much for your help and contribution!

To my mother-in-law Julia: Thank you for always being my #1 beta reader. It wouldn't be nearly as fun to do what I do without you.

ABOUT THE AUTHOR

Sophie Mays is a contemporary romance author who focuses on inspirational stories with heartwarmingly happy outcomes. Believing that we are all put on this Earth with a purpose, no matter how big or small it seems, Sophie knows that without a doubt each and every one of our contributions is essential to making the world go round. After many years of writing, and doing a great deal of soul-searching on the side, she found that her contribution was the thing that was obvious to all...she was through and through, devoted to bringing hope, happiness and motivating inspiration to everyone around her. Whether through her books or her personal relationships, Sophie has always been known for her dogged dedication to making people believe that anything is possible if you truly believe and put your faith in up above.

Aside from being a full-time writer and optimist, Sophie maintains an impressive collection of magazines (piles of Southern Living and Real Simple are constantly being recycled by her husband), she is addicted to audio books, loves inspirational podcasts, and scours the globe (aka recipe books) in search of the perfect "healthy" dessert to bring to parties. She lives in the coastal South, where she feels lucky to get the best of both worlds: the sound of rolling waves, salty air, lemonade tea, and sweet Southern charm.

Visit www.LoveLifeFaith.com to learn more

Also By Love Light Faith Publishing

Enjoy Inspirational Clean Fiction & Romance books, including the following:

Contemporary Romance

For Love…and Donuts (Book 1) - Sophie Mays

Scottish Holiday - Sophie Mays

A Whole Latte Christmas - Sophie Mays

Key West Christmas - Sophie Mays

Regency Romance

A Lady's Reluctant Heart - Caroline Johnson

Historical Romance

A Christmas Journey Home - Caroline Johnson

Amish Romance

A Simple Heart's Journey Home - Sunny Brooks

Please join the Love Light Faith Mailing List at www.LoveLightFaith.com to be notified of upcoming releases and promotions!

11629164R00079

Printed in Great Britain
by Amazon